First published in Great Britain by HarperCollins Publishers Ltd in 1997

5 7 9 10 8 6

ISBN: 0 00 198259-1

Cover design and illustrations by County Studios
A CIP catalogue for this title is available from the British Library.

Printed and bound in Singapore

NODDY™

BEDTIME STORIES

Enid Blyton™

Collins

An Imprint of HarperCollinsPublishers

THIS BOOK BELONGS TO

CONTENTS

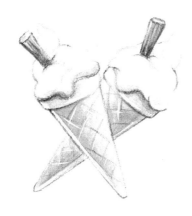

A letter from Noddy

Hallo, Boys and Girls,

Guess who I am? Yes, I'm little Noddy, and if you come to Toy Town where I live, you will always know when I'm coming because my blue hat has a bell on the top which goes jingle-jingle-jing.

If you want to visit me I live in my dear little house of bricks called "House-for-One". Next door live Mr and Mrs Tubby Bear and they are very kind to me. I have a little red and yellow car of my own because I'm a taxi driver and I work very hard. Sometimes I go to the wood to see my dear friend Big-Ears the Brownie. He lives in a Toadstool House with his cat and he has a bicycle with a bell on it.

You can meet more of my friends and share in our many adventures in my story collection. I hope you will enjoy it. Now I will sign my name in my Very Best Writing.

Love from

Noddy

WHAT A THING TO HAPPEN

Once Noddy had a bear on wheels for a passenger. He was a nice bear, but because he was on wheels he found it rather difficult to sit in the car.

"I'm not sure I want you for a passenger," said Noddy, at last, after he had spent five minutes trying to fix the bear in safely. "You'll scratch my car with your wheels."

"Oh, please do take me," said the bear. "I've got to go and have my growl seen to. It's gone wrong. I do beg of you to take me, because I'm not allowed on the bus."

"All right," said Noddy, "I'll take you. But really you are a most awkward passenger to fit in!" They set off at last.

The bear wanted to go to Bear Town and that was quite a long way off. And, dear me, halfway there something peculiar happened!

When Noddy drove over a big bump in the road one of the wheels flew off his little car! It came right off and rolled at top speed down the hill behind them. The car gave a jolt and came to a stop on only three wheels.

"Oh, I say! A wheel's gone!" said Noddy, looking scared. "What am I to do?"

"Go after it," said the bear. "I'll get out and look too. You can ride on my back if you like because I can run very quickly downhill on my four big wheels."

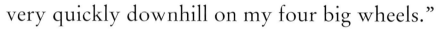

So Noddy got on the bear's furry back and away they went down the hill to look for the lost wheel. But they couldn't find it anywhere! It had quite disappeared.

"Fallen in the river, I suppose, or been eaten by a goat," said the bear.

"Do goats eat wheels?" said Noddy, in surprise. "Oh, I shall never like goats again."

They went back to the car. "Well, we'll have to leave my poor little car here all by itself because its spare wheel is at the garage, being mended," said Noddy, with tears in his eyes. "It won't like being left. It'll miss its own garage."

"I've got an idea," said the bear, "but I don't know if you'll think it's a very good one. I suppose you wouldn't like me to lend you one of *my* wheels, would you? They're about the same size as the car's wheels, and one of mine might just do for it till the other wheel is found or you get a new one."

"Well, what a wonderful idea!" cried Noddy. He undid one of the bear's wheels, and he and the bear together fitted it on the car. It wasn't quite the same size, but it did very well indeed.

"The car goes along rather jerkily," said Noddy, "but, anyway, it *goes*! You really are a clever bear. I'm so glad I took you for a passenger after all."

"Yes, you were kind, and kindness is always a very good thing," said the bear. "Well, here we are at Bear Town. I'll get my growl put right and then we'll go back. I think I can run on three wheels all right."

He was soon back, with his growl nice and deep again. He growled just to show Noddy how good it was. Then Noddy helped him into the car again and off they went.

"You'd better come and have some lemonade and buns with me," said Noddy, when they got back. "Bears do like buns, don't they?"

"Oh yes," said the bear, pleased. So Noddy drove the little car to his house - and there, leaning by the front gate, was the lost wheel! Noddy stared at it in wonder and delight.

"Somebody brought your wheel back for you," said Mr Tubby, the bear, looking out of one of his windows. "I told him to put it there, and I gave him a penny for bringing it. I say, that's a very odd wheel you've got instead!"

"It may be odd, but it's been very useful!" said Noddy. "Now, bear, you can have your wheel back, and I can put mine on again. What a bit of luck!"

They did enjoy their buns and lemonade. When the bear went he said thank you to Noddy. "And if EVER you want a spare wheel in a hurry again, let me know. I'll always lend you one of mine!" he said.

Wasn't it nice of him!

NODDY IS RATHER CLEVER

One day Mr Noah was worried. He had counted the animals and birds in his Ark, and, dear me, two were missing!

"The two brown bears are gone," he said. "Now what shall I do? How very naughty of them."

He went to tell Mr Plod, and soon everyone knew that the two brown bears had run away from the Ark.

"Just because I said they were to wipe their feet when they came into the Ark after their walk!" said Mrs Noah. "Really, they are too touchy for words!"

"Who's going after them?" said Mr Plod. "I hear they can be rather fierce. I have too much to do today to chase them myself. Look, there's Big-Ears. Perhaps he would go after them. Hey, Big-Ears!"

Big-Ears said he would rush round and about on his little bicycle and see if he could find the bears. "I'll tell Noddy, too," he said. "He is out in his car this morning. He can look out for them."

He found Noddy and told him. Noddy felt rather scared. "But I don't *want* to chase bears," he said. "They are *much* more likely to chase me. And what would I do if I saw them? I might run away."

"Don't be such a little coward," said Big-Ears. "Anyway, you'll be in your car. You'll be quite safe."

He rode away on his bicycle and Noddy went off in his car, hoping that he wouldn't see a single bear. The wooden bears from the Ark always looked rather fierce to him.

And, will you believe it, as he turned a corner, there were the two bears walking down the lane! Noddy was full of alarm. *Now* what was he to do? Should he turn round at top speed and rush away?

No. That wouldn't be at all brave. Big-Ears would be most ashamed of him. Noddy stopped his car and stared at the two brown bears coming towards him. His little knees shook in fright.

And then a Wonderful Idea came into Noddy's head, and the little bell on his hat tinkled loudly. It always did when Noddy had a good idea.

He called to the two brown bears. "Hey! Do you want a lift?"

"Well, we *are* rather tired," said one bear. "Yes, we'd like a lift."

So they both got into the car, and it really was a terrible squash. But the bears seemed very grateful and friendly, so Noddy didn't mind.

He drove off at top speed. Where was Noddy going? Ah, that was his Wonderful Idea!

"I shall drive at top speed to Mr Noah at the Ark!" thought Noddy. "Yes, that's what I shall do. Oh, what a Wonderful Idea!"

Along the lane, and over the bridge, and through the village. Parp-parp-parp went the hooter, and everyone turned and stared.

"Look! There's Noddy! He's caught the two runaway bears!" shouted Big-Ears, wobbling along on his bicycle.

"He's got the bears!" yelled Mr Tubby.

"Isn't he brave?" shouted Mr Plod.

Big-Ears followed on his bicycle. Noddy drove up to the Ark - and there was Mr Noah standing at the door, waiting. He looked very stern.

The bears stared in surprise. "Oh - we've come to the Ark," they said.

"You have," said Mr Noah. "Get out of that car. Go into the Ark at once. And be sure to WIPE YOUR FEET. Then put yourselves to bed in disgrace. I will come and talk to you soon."

The bears hung their heads and shuffled off into the Ark. Big-Ears rode up, panting. He leapt off his bicycle and thumped Noddy on the back.

"You're a wonder!" he said. "You're a marvel! Isn't he, Mr Noah?"

"Yes," said Mr Noah, "and very very brave, too. Noddy, you shall have the biggest ice-cream you've ever seen!"

So he did - and you can see him eating it. Isn't it ENORMOUS!

A-Tishoo!

"A-tish-oooo!" said Noddy suddenly, and tried to catch the sneeze in his hanky.

"You've caught a cold," said Big-Ears.

"I haven't," said Noddy. "I think it must have caught *me*, Big-Ears. Oh dear, I hope I shan't give it to you, too. A-TISH-ooooo!"

"Now, you go to bed, and get a hot-water bottle, and wrap yourself up in a shawl, and have something hot to drink with a lemon in it," said Big-Ears. "You'll soon be better then."

Well, Noddy didn't give his cold to Big-Ears, he gave it away somewhere else! He was driving his car along when suddenly it made a most peculiar noise.

"Whoooooooosh-OOOO!" It shook and shivered and Noddy was quite alarmed.

"What are you doing, car? Have you got a puncture in one of your tyres?"

"WHOOOOOSH-OOO!" said the car, even more loudly, and shook and shivered again.

"I believe you're sneezing. I believe you've got a cold," said Noddy anxiously. "Oh dear, oh dear. Well, I must look after you well, because it would never do to have a car that coughed and sneezed all the time. Come along home - I'll put you to bed."

Well, Noddy took his little car home and put it into the garage. He fetched a big blanket and draped it all round it, like a shawl.

"Is that nice and warm?" he said. "Now I'll get you a hot drink with lemon in."

Off he went and boiled a kettle of water and poured it into a jug with hot lemon in it. Then out he went to the garage and put the hot drink into the car's water-tank. It seemed to like it very much.

"Now for a hot-water bottle," said Noddy, and bustled off again. Soon he had the bottle ready and he put it just underneath the car to keep it warm.

"You'll soon be all right,"

he said. "Now keep warm, go to sleep, and wake up better in the morning because we've got a lot of passengers to take out."

Well, the car did go to sleep. It began to snore a little because it was so warm and comfortable. Mr Tubby Bear was coming home late that night and he was most surprised to hear this strange noise coming from Noddy's garage. He peeped down and looked through the keyhole.

And there was the car, fast asleep, warm, comfortable and snoring a little. Mr Tubby couldn't help smiling.

"Dear old Noddy!" he said. "He even tries to make his car comfortable and happy. I suppose it's got a cold! Well, it should be better tomorrow, with all this kind treatment."

It was, of course. It didn't sneeze any more, and it didn't cough once. "There," said Noddy, as he drove away in it to collect his passengers, "see how clever I am, little car! I can even cure your cold!"

A LITTLE MISTAKE

Once little Noddy went to tea with Big-Ears. He drove up to his toadstool house, and hooted loudly.

"Parp-parp!"

Big-Ears came to the door. "Hallo, little Noddy! You're in good time. I've almost got tea ready, and there is a lovely new pot of honey!"

"Oooh!" said Noddy. "I like honey. I wish I were a bee. I'd like to be small enough to go and hunt for honey in the flowers whenever I was hungry."

He went into Big-Ears' little house. It was such a dear little house, and so cosy inside. Noddy loved it. Big-Ears had laid the table, and there was a plate of new bread and butter, a big pot of honey, a round fruit cake and ginger biscuits.

"Now sit down and tell me all your news," said Big-Ears. "Have you had any passengers in your car today?"

"Yes, two," said little Noddy. "One was big Mr Jumbo, and he's so heavy he makes the tyres go quite flat. And the other was Sally Skittle, and two little girl-skittles. Oh dear - one fell out, and Sally Skittle was cross."

"Well, skittles are always falling down," said Big-Ears. "That's what they're meant to do. Look, Noddy - I've spread a whole big slice of bread and butter with honey for you. Here you are."

"Oh, thank you, Big-Ears," said Noddy, and reached out his hand for

for it. "Oh, goodness me - I've put my thumb on the honey. Can I lick it, or is that rude?"

"Get your hanky out, Noddy," said Big-Ears, "I know what you're like with honey! You'll have it all over yourself in a minute!"

Noddy put his hand in his pocket, and pulled out - a letter! He stared at it in surprise.

"This isn't my hanky," he said. "Dear me, where did this letter come from?"

Big-Ears looked at it. "It's addressed to Miss Jane Jumbo," he said. "How odd!"

"Oh, I remember now - oh dear! Mr Jumbo asked me to post it for him!" said Noddy, his head nodding madly. "I forgot. I quite forgot!"

"Then that was very bad of you," said Big-Ears. "If you say you will do something you MUST do it. Now, you go straight out to the little red post-box down the lane, and post that letter right away. No, you can't finish your tea first. Go now."

"All right," said Noddy, seeing that Big-Ears looked quite cross with

him. "May I take my piece of bread and butter and honey with me, Big-Ears, please?"

"Yes," said Big-Ears. "Hurry up. I'll wait till you come back before I cut the fruit cake."

Noddy hurried off down the lane, his slice of bread and honey in one hand and the letter in the other.

Big-Ears sat and waited.

And then he heard a noise. What was it? Good gracious, it was Noddy, and he was wailing loudly as he came back from the post. Big-Ears rushed to the door.

"Noddy! What's the matter? Have you hurt yourself?"

"Big-Ears - oh Big-Ears - when I got to the post-box, I - I - I..." wept Noddy.

"Well, go on," said Big-Ears.

"Oh, Big-Ears, I made a mistake - and I posted my bread and honey!" wailed Noddy. "I did, I did! And I made another mistake too. I bit a big piece out of Mr Jumbo's letter. Look!"

Big-Ears looked at the bitten letter. Then he looked at Noddy. "Well, well, well - whatever will you do next?" he said. "Posting bread and honey - and eating letters!"

"Go and get my bread and honey!" wept Noddy.

"I can't because the post-box is locked," said Big-Ears. "You'll have to go and tell the postman you are sorry, when he comes to collect the letters. And you'll have to go and tell Mr Jumbo what you have done, and say you're sorry to him too. He'll have to write another letter."

"But they'll both be so cross with me," said Noddy, and oh dear, he wiped his eyes with Jumbo's letter!

"That's not your hanky!" said Big-Ears. "Noddy, people ought to be cross with you when you're silly. Now, you go straight off to Mr Jumbo's. Hurry! You can have your tea when you come back!"

So there goes poor little Noddy in his car, feeling very sorry for himself. Fancy posting a slice of bread and honey - what a thing to do!

BIG-EARS' RED HAT

Big-Ears always wore a red hat. It fitted him well and had a nice point at the top. He was very proud of it and wore it every day.

One day Noddy called for him in his little car and said he would take him for a ride. "I haven't any passengers today," he said, "so you can come for a little trip with me, Big-Ears. I will show you how fast my little car can go."

Big-Ears was pleased. He got in and Noddy set off through the wood. Parp-parp! Parp-parp! He hooted his horn to make the rabbits get out of the way.

When he got to a hill Noddy went down it very fast indeed. Whoooooosh! Big-Ears felt the wind rushing by his head, and he put up his hand to hold onto his hat.

But alas! It flew right off his head and up into the air! Big-Ears gave a yell.

"Stop, stop, Noddy! Stop, I say!"

"Oh, we can't stop in the middle of a hill," said Noddy, who was really enjoying himself. "It's all right, Big-Ears. Don't be frightened. I'm really a very good driver."

"I'm NOT frightened!" said Big-Ears crossly. "But I want you to STOP. Can't you see that my hat has blown away?"

Noddy turned to look, and was so surprised to see Big-Ears without his red hat that he let the car almost run into a lamp-post. Big-Ears clutched the wheel just in time.

"Noddy! Look where you are going!"

"Well, you told me to look and see that your hat was gone," said Noddy. "I can't look two ways at once. Oh, Big-Ears - your lovely hat!"

27

"Yes. My lovely hat!" said Big-Ears. "I shall never, never get another one to fit my big head. That was specially made for me. How silly you are to go so fast, Noddy."

"We'll go back and look for it," said Noddy, and he turned the car round. Back they went, chugging up the hill. Then Noddy suddenly gave a shout.

"There it is, look - on that bush over there! I'll get it." So out he got, and ran to a clump of bushes. All sorts of things had been draped over them - a blue dress, a pink petticoat, a yellow shawl - but Noddy only had eyes for the little red thing on the smallest bush. He pounced on it.

And then a cross voice called out to him.

"Hey, you little robber! What are you doing, taking my washing! I've just hung it over the bushes to dry. You leave it alone!"

"But it's Big-Ears' hat," said Noddy.

"It is not," said a plump mother-doll running over to him. "It's my red scarf!"

And, dear me, so it was! Noddy shook it out and it wasn't a red hat at all, but just a pretty scarf. He was most surprised. He ran back to the car with the mother-doll after him.

"I'm sorry, I'm sorry, I'm sorry!" he shouted, and drove off at top speed. Big-Ears looked very cross.

"We shall never find my hat," he said. "I don't feel as if I want to speak to you today, Noddy. I'm annoyed with you."

Noddy hated Big-Ears not to speak to him. He looked all round and about for the lost red hat. Ah - there it was, blowing over the grass in a nearby field.

Noddy hopped out of the car and ran to it. The wind played a fine game with him! It blew the red thing here and there, and Noddy went up to his knees in a stream before he caught it.

And it wasn't the hat after all - it was just an old red rag that Mrs Skittle had thrown away on her rubbish-heap.

The wind had taken it to play with.

Noddy went sadly back to the car. Big-Ears didn't say a word. He just sat and stared in front of him. It was really dreadful.

Noddy sighed and started the car again. If only he could find Big-Ears' hat! Then everything would be all right again.

And then he really *did* see a red hat! It was sticking up just over the top of a low hedge. The wind must have taken it there! Noddy leapt out of the car and ran to it. Yes, it really was a red, pointed hat.

He tugged at it and it came easily into his hand. But, dear me, somebody on the other side of the hedge suddenly stood up and looked over the top, very angry indeed. It was Mr Big-Beard, an old brownie.

"Noddy! How DARE you! Snatching my hat off my head just as I was taking a nap under the hedge in the sun! I've a mind to tell Mr Plod. Come here!"

"I'm sorry, I'm sorry, I'm sorry!" wailed poor Noddy. He threw back the hat and ran to the car. Oh dear - what a dreadful thing to happen. And there was Big-Ears, still cross and not saying a word.

"I'll drive you home, Big-Ears," said Noddy, in a very small voice. "This is not my lucky morning." So he drove Big-Ears slowly home - and, will you believe it, when they got there, there was something red on the top of Big-Ears' chimney. How they stared!

"It's my hat!" said Big-Ears joyfully. "The wind brought it back for me, and because I wasn't in it put it on my chimney where I could see it! Oh, what a lucky thing!"

"I'll get a ladder and take it down for you, dear Big-Ears," said Noddy. "And then you will speak to me nicely again, won't you?"

So he got Big-Ears' red hat for him, and Big-Ears smiled and put it on. Then he put his arm round little Noddy and squeezed him.

"I'm sorry I was cross," he said. "I'm always cross without my hat."

"Then you must never, never lose it again," said Noddy happily. And Big-Ears said he never, never would!

NODDY GETS A FRIGHT

Once Noddy was asked to a party. Sally Skittle asked him, and Noddy was very pleased.

"I'm going to Sam Skittle's party," he told Big-Ears. "His mother asked me if I would. It's his birthday."

"Then you must take him a present," said Big-Ears. "Have you any money in your money-box, Noddy?"

"Oh yes, lots!" said Noddy. "I was saving up to buy myself a nice pair of warm gloves, Big-Ears. My hands do get so cold on these winter days, when I'm driving the car."

Big-Ears tipped out the money from the money-box. "Yes," he said, "you've quite a lot. You can buy the gloves and a birthday present for Sam Skittle, too."

So Noddy bought Sam Skittle a little trumpet, and he bought himself a pair of fine red gloves, very warm indeed.

He felt very proud when he put
them on. They were the first pair he
had had. He thought he would wear
them to the party and drive
himself there in his little car.

"Now - am I all clean and
tidy?" he said to himself
when the party afternoon
came. "Have I washed my
hands and face? Yes, I have.
Have I brushed my hair?
Yes - oh no, I haven't.
Dear me, what a good thing
that I ask myself questions
like these!"

He brushed his hair. He put on
his hat, and the little bell jingled merrily.
He tied up his shoe-laces well and brushed some dust off his shorts.
He put on his nice new gloves and went out to his car.

"I've got new gloves that fit my wooden hands nicely," said Noddy
to his car.

"Parp-parp!" said the car, and off they went. Soon they came to
Sally Skittle's house and Noddy got out and went in at the gate - and,
dear me, on the path was an ENORMOUS puddle left by the rain!
Noddy stepped right into it. Splash!

"Oh - how wet my shoes are!" he said. "What will Sally Skittle say!"

Sally Skittle scolded him. "Dear dear! To think you didn't see a puddle as big as that!" she said. "And will you believe it, Billy Bear has done just the same! Take off your shoes, and I will dry them. Give me your gloves, too, and I will put them with your shoes."

So Noddy and Billy Bear didn't wear any shoes at the party, but they enjoyed it all the same. The floor was nice and slippery and the two of them slid up and down.

The tea was lovely and the cake was lovely too - the candles were made in the shape of skittles, and that made everyone laugh.

Sam Skittle liked the trumpet that Noddy brought him. Sally Skittle, his Mother, said that he liked it too much, because he wouldn't stop blowing it!

Noddy was sorry when it was time to go home. "I like the beginning of a party, and I like the middle, but I don't like the end," he said. "Why don't we have parties with only beginnings and middles, Sally Skittle?"

"Now, don't you begin asking me silly questions like Sam," said Sally. "Look, go and find your shoes, Noddy. There they are, over there, with your red gloves."

Billy Bear said he couldn't be bothered to put his on. "I'll tie my shoes round my neck and stuff my gloves into my pocket," he said.

Noddy put on the red shoes with blue laces. He didn't put on his gloves till he had shaken hands with Sally Skittle.

"Thank you very much for having me," he said. "I have had a lovely time."

Then out he went to his little car. He put on his gloves, and off he went.

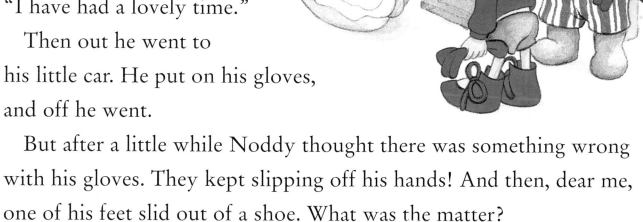

But after a little while Noddy thought there was something wrong with his gloves. They kept slipping off his hands! And then, dear me, one of his feet slid out of a shoe. What was the matter?

Noddy stopped the car and got out. He put on the shoe again - but

his foot seemed much too small for it! No wonder it slipped off - and, goodness his hands were much too small for his gloves, too!

"I'm going small!" suddenly wailed Noddy. "Somebody's put a spell on me! I'm going smaller and smaller, I know I am! Soon I'll be so small that I won't be seen - and then what shall I do? I'll go and tell Big-Ears!"

So he got into his car again and drove at top speed to Big-Ears' little toadstool house. He jumped out of his car and ran to Big-Ears' door, one of his shoes falling off as he ran.

"Big-Ears! Big-Ears! Something dreadful is happening!" wailed Noddy, knocking at the door. "I'm going small. Ever so small. Look at my new gloves - they just won't keep on my hands - and look at my feet! My shoes won't stay on!"

"Good gracious! This is dreadful!" said Big-Ears in alarm. "But wait - your hat still fits your head! You can't be going small. Give me one of the shoes, Noddy."

Noddy gave him one, and after one look at it Big-Ears began to laugh and laugh. "Oh, Noddy! HOW silly you are! These are Billy Bear's shoes. Look, his name is inside - and his gloves, too! He has enormous feet and paws - so, of course, his gloves and shoes don't fit you!"

Dear me, Noddy was so very very glad! And see, off he goes to Mrs Tubby Bear's to get back his own shoes and gloves. He isn't going small after all!

BIG-EARS' UMBRELLA

Now once Big-Ears was very cross because it was raining and he wanted to go shopping and couldn't find his umbrella.

"I lent it to Noddy - and he didn't bring it back," thought Big-Ears. "Really, that's *very* naughty of him. Well, I must just take my old umbrella, though it's full of holes."

So he walked through the wood and down to Toy Village holding the old umbrella over his head. He did his shopping and soon filled his big square basket.

Then he set off home again. When he turned a corner he saw something rather peculiar in front of him. It was a very big umbrella over a very small person - whose legs were all that showed below the umbrella!

"Ha! That's my big new umbrella!" thought Big-Ears. "The one I lent Noddy. And those are his legs below it - I know his red shoes and blue laces! Now - where's he going with my umbrella, the little rascal!"

Well, Noddy was going to Big-Ears' house up in the wood! When he saw that it was raining that morning, he suddenly remembered that he hadn't taken back Big-Ears' umbrella.

"Oh dear - Big-Ears will want to go shopping today and he'll get SO wet!" thought Noddy. "And he'll be very, very cross with me for not taking it back before. He always says I should return borrowed things AT ONCE!"

So there he was, almost hidden by the big umbrella, on his way to Big-Ears' home. And there was Big-Ears behind him, laughing at Noddy's feet going in and out under the enormous umbrella.

"Little monkey - little scamp - only taking back my umbrella when it's pouring with rain!" thought Big-Ears. "Well - I'll make him carry my shopping for me all the way home!"

So what do you think he did?

On the top of the big umbrella was a large spike, sticking upwards - and Big-Ears very carefully placed his basket upon it! The spike held the basket firmly, and as Big-Ears had carefully covered up his shopping it wouldn't get wet!

"Dear me!" said Noddy to himself, "this umbrella suddenly feels VERY heavy! I wish it would stop raining - then I could put it down."

But the rain still poured down, and little Noddy staggered on, holding the umbrella over him, with the basket of shopping balanced on top, the spike holding it nice and firm.

Big-Ears walked behind, chuckling. He knew that the basket would feel very heavy, but it would certainly teach Noddy a lesson! On they went, up the path through the woods, and Noddy didn't even guess that Big-Ears was so close behind him!

"Hallo, little Noddy!" said Big-Ears, when they reached his house. "I see you've got my umbrella."

"Oh Big-Ears - you made me jump!" said Noddy. "Have you been shopping? Oh Big-Ears, I hope you didn't get wet. I've brought back your umbrella, and if I'd known you were shopping in the village I'd have carried your basket home for you too, to show you I was sorry I forgot about your umbrella."

"Well - never mind - you have carried it home!" said Big-Ears. "No - don't put the umbrella down - give it to me. There - look - my basket is on the umbrella spike - you carried it all the way!"

"Oh! No wonder I thought your umbrella was heavy!" cried Noddy. "Oh Big-Ears, you won't be cross about your umbrella now, will you - because I did carry your shopping all the way home!"

"No. I'm not cross," said Big-Ears. "But I shall be NEXT time you forget to bring back something you borrow."

"You won't - because I shan't forget, Big-Ears!" said Noddy. "I shan't - I really SHAN'T!"

BUMPITY BUMPITY BUMP!

"Hey, Noddy, hey! Take me to the market!" shouted a teddy bear who was standing at the corner of the street with a sack as Noddy came by in his little car.

Noddy stopped. "Hallo, Mr Bear," he said. "Get in. Put your sack at the back."

"What do you charge to go to the market?" asked the bear. Noddy didn't like him very much. He was rather dirty and his coat was torn.

"Sixpence," said Noddy, setting off. They hadn't gone very far before Noddy heard a little noise behind - bump - bumpity, bump.

"What's that?" he said.

"Oh, nothing," said the bear. "The road is so bumpy that the car makes quite a noise."

"All the same I'm sure I can hear something going bumpity-bump," said Noddy. "As if something was falling down from the car. I do hope it's not falling to bits."

"Of course not," said the bear. "Please don't stop, Noddy - I really must get to market quickly. I've some *beautiful* big apples in my sack, freshly picked this morning and I'm going to sell them for a lot of money."

Now the bear was telling a naughty story. He *hadn't* got apples in his bag! He only had potatoes, and not very good ones either! He also had something else in that sack - a big hole! He had cut one there himself, so that the potatoes would fall out one by one as Noddy took him along in his little car. What a peculiar thing to do!

They came to the market and then Mr Bear got out and went to collect his sack. He gave a loud yell.

"What's the matter?" said Noddy, anxiously.

"My apples! My BEAUTIFUL apples! There's not a single one left in the sack!" cried Mr. Bear. "Not one. They must have fallen out every time you went over a bump, Noddy. That's the worst of a silly car like this - it has such bad springs that not even apples in a sack are safe!"

"My car is a very good one!" said Noddy, fiercely. "I *heard* something falling into the road, but you wouldn't let me stop. I'm sorry about it, but it's NOT my fault!"

"It *is*," said Mr Bear, looking very fierce too. "Because of your silly bumpy car I've lost all my apples - and I would have sold them for twenty shillings."

"You would not," said Noddy.

"I would," said Mr Bear. "But as I don't expect you've got much money, I will only charge you ten shillings for losing them out of your car."

"Ten shillings! I've only got *two* shillings!" said Noddy. "And I'm not going to give you that. *You* owe me sixpence for taking you to the market!"

"We'll tell Mr Plod," said Mr Bear, and he beckoned to the policeman, who was standing in the market, directing traffic.

Mr Plod listened to Mr Bear's tale. "ALL my beautiful apples gone!" he wailed. "And all because of his bumpy car. I'm very kind only to charge him ten shillings."

"You must pay up, Noddy," said Mr Plod. "Pay the two shillings you have and..."

Just then Big-Ears rode up panting on his bicycle. He had a very big basket in front, because it was his shopping day. It was full to the brim with old potatoes.

"Hey, Noddy!" he called. "I've been trying to catch you up for ages. I was riding behind your car and I saw these potatoes falling out of a sack at the back. So I picked them up, put them in my basket - and here they are. You must have a big hole in that sack!"

"*Potatoes*!" cried Noddy. "But Mr Bear said they were his very best apples. Oooh, you fibber, Mr Bear!"

Mr Plod suddenly caught hold of Mr Bear.

"Ha!" he said. "This needs looking into! You've been tricking our little Noddy - you put old potatoes into a sack with a hole in it and said they were good apples. You're a bad bear. Now you just pay Noddy a whole shilling for his trouble, put your old potatoes into your sack and carry them away to the rubbish-heap!"

Mr Bear looked scared. He gave Noddy a shilling, and Big-Ears emptied the potatoes into the sack. Mr Bear put it on his back without a word and walked off with it.

Bumpity-bump! Bump-bump-bump!

Noddy gave a squeal of laughter. "Oh! He won't get far before his sack feels as light as can be! There go all his potatoes out of the hole, one by one!"

Bumpity-bump! It serves you right, Mr Bear. You shouldn't play horrid tricks on people.

"Big-Ears, thank you very much!" said little Noddy. "I've got a shilling instead of a sixpence! Let's go and spend it on ice-creams!"

So off they go together. Good old Big-Ears - he really is a help to little Noddy, isn't he?

NODDY AND THE FIRE-ENGINE

One afternoon, when Noddy was driving slowly through Toy Village, he noticed a very peculiar thing.

A little house stood back from the road with a nice garden in front - and out of one of the upstairs windows was coming a thin spiral of smoke.

Noddy stared at it as he drove by. Why should smoke come out of a *window*? Hadn't the house got any chimneys? Yes, it had four! Then why did the smoke come out of a window?

"I wonder - I just *wonder* - if there's something on fire there!" said Noddy, and he suddenly felt excited and his bell rang loudly on his hat. "Perhaps I'd better knock at the door and ask if everything is all right."

So he drove back to the gate of the pretty little house. He got out of his car and went up the garden path. He knocked loudly at the blue front door and rang the bell. Rat-a-tat-tat! Jingle-jing!

Nobody came to the door, so Noddy went round the back. The kitchen door was locked and he couldn't make anyone hear - nor could he get in.

Then he saw a little note on the doorstep. "No bread today. Back tomorrow."

"Oh - the people have gone away!" said Noddy. "NOW what shall I do? I really must find out if something is on fire."

He went round to the front again, and saw that a tree grew right up to the window out of which the smoke was drifting. "I'd better climb it," said Noddy. "It doesn't look a hard tree to climb."

So up he went and looked in at the window, which was shut except for a little crack at the top. Goodness - what a shock he had! A fire had been left burning in the room, and a piece of coal had jumped out on to the rug and was burning!

"Fire!" shouted Noddy, and almost fell out of the tree. "Fetch the fire-engine, quick! The rug's burning - and now the flame has reached a little table and one leg's burning! Fire!"

He tried to open the window a little more, to get in and throw the burning things out of the window - but he couldn't. Oh dear, oh dear -

the flames were now burning all the table, and a waste paper basket too - and soon they would reach the book-shelf and what a blaze there would be then!

"I must go to the fire-station and tell the firemen," thought Noddy. "Yes, that's what I must do."

So he slid down the tree and got into his car. Away he went, hooting madly to make everyone get out of his way quickly. Mr Plod saw him flash by and was very cross.

"Going along at sixty miles an hour!" said Mr. Plod. "I'll have something to say to you about this, Noddy."

Noddy arrived at the fire-station - but alas, the fire-engine wasn't there, nor were there any firemen to be seen.

"Where's everybody," yelled Noddy. "Fire, fire!"

A small beetle shouted back to Noddy. "They've taken the fire-engine to put out a fire on Farmer Straw's rick."

"Oh, goodness me!" said Noddy and raced his car up to the farm. Ah - there was the fire-engine standing quietly in the lane. The fire had been put out in the rick - but where were the firemen? Not one was to be seen!

"Fire! Fire!" shouted Noddy. The firemen were all down at the farm-house having some lemonade and cakes with the farmer and his wife. One put his head out of the door when he heard Noddy shout. He put it back again, laughing heartily.

"It's only little Noddy! He's seen our fire-engine and he's got all excited. He's shouting "Fire! Fire!" as if there really was one here!"

Noddy was very worried indeed. He couldn't *think* where the firemen had gone to. What was he to do?

"That dear little house will be all burnt down if I go to look for the firemen," he thought. "Oh - I wonder now - I do, do wonder - if *I* could drive that fire-engine!"

He slid out of his little car and ran to the gleaming fire-engine.

He climbed into the driving seat. Now - here was the steering-wheel - and there was the thing that started up the engine - and that must be the brake - he could only *just* reach it because his legs were so short.

R-r-r-r-r-r! He started up the engine - it moved off down the lane. Ooooooh! What a thrill for Noddy! His head nodded madly and his face went very red.

The fire-bell rang as he went along - and when he came into Toy Village everyone ran out to see the fire-engine, Mr Plod too. He stared with his mouth wide open at the surprising sight of *Noddy* driving the fire-engine!

"What next?" he said. "What next?" And he jumped on his bicycle and raced after Noddy.

Noddy came to the house where the fire was, and stopped the fire-engine. Dear me, there was a *great* deal of smoke coming out of the window now - and was that a flame?

Noddy leapt down and wondered how to get the hose and the water to the house. What did firemen do next? But he didn't have to wonder long because here came Mr Plod on his bicycle, red in the face with anger.

"What do you mean by this, little Noddy?" he roared - and then he suddenly saw all the thick smoke coming out of the window.

"See - it's on fire!" shouted Noddy. "I found the fire-engine but I couldn't see the firemen - so I brought the engine here myself, Mr Plod. How do we get the water to put out the fire?"

Well, Mr Plod knew all about things like that of course! A lot of people had come running up now, and he gave his orders quickly.

"You, Mr Straw, find the water under that iron grating there - take up the lid, that's right. And you, Mr Toy Dog, fasten the end of that hose to the tap down there.

"Turn on the water when I tell you! Hey, Mr Noah, help me to run the hose into the garden."

Noddy climbed the tree and looked in at the window. "Everything's burning!" he cried. "Bring the hose up here, Mr Plod. Shall I break the window?"

"Yes!" shouted Mr Plod, and CRASH, Noddy broke the window so that the hose could go through. He pulled up the hose himself, and then Tessie Bear climbed up beside him, and soon the water was pouring into the burning room, making a hissing, sizzling noise.

"Hurray!" shouted everyone. "Hurray! The fire will soon be out!"

"It's OUT!" shouted Noddy. "Nothing but smoke left."

"Come on down, Noddy," said Mr Plod, and Noddy climbed down, keeping as far away from Mr Plod as he could. But the policeman grabbed hold of him - and will you believe it, he set little Noddy on his shoulder and carried him all the way through Toy Village like that.

"Here comes Noddy, who saved a house from burning down!" he shouted. "Here comes Noddy, who drove the fire-engine all by himself - though he mustn't do it again unless he asks me. Here comes Noddy, so give him a cheer!"

And you should have heard the loud hurrays all the way down the street.

Big-Ears couldn't *think* what was going on when he came riding through on his bicycle.

When he saw Noddy being carried on Mr Plod's shoulder he was so astonished that he fell off his bicycle - bump!

"Noddy! What are you doing up there? Noddy, why are you so dirty, why is your face so black? Noddy why..."

You wait a little, Big-Ears, and hear Noddy answer your questions. You really WILL be surprised!

BOTHER YOU, MR JUMBO

Every day Mr Jumbo went to the station and caught the train. He was lazy and he liked to go to the station in Noddy's car.

"I don't like taking you, Mr Jumbo," Noddy said. "You're so heavy that you make the car go right down on your side, and you're so big that you squash me dreadfully. Please, I'd rather not take you."

But he had to, because whenever Noddy was in the ice-cream shop, which was next door to Mr Jumbo's house, Mr Jumbo came out of his front door and got into Noddy's car, which was parked outside.

Noddy kept finding him there, and then, of course, he had to drive him to the station.

One morning Noddy had done some shopping and he put his packet of butter on the seat beside him. Then he drove to the ice-cream shop and went inside. Out came Mr Jumbo, got into the car - and sat down heavily on the butter!

Noddy came running out. "Mr Jumbo! Did you move my butter? Oh, don't say you're sitting on it!"

Well, he was, of course - and when he got out at the station the butter looked exactly as if a big steam-roller had been over it and rolled it thin and flat. How upset Noddy was!

Now will you believe it, the very next day poor Noddy left six eggs in a bag on the seat of his car - and as soon as Mr Jumbo saw Noddy going into the ice-cream shop, out he came, got into the car - and sat down on the eggs!

When Noddy came out he saw yellow yolk dripping out of the side of the car, and he knew what had happened. Oh *dear*!

"Mr Jumbo! All my breakfast eggs were on that seat," said Noddy, almost crying. "Why don't you look on the seat before you get in? You're SILLY!"

"If you talk to me like that I'll bounce up and down," said Mr Jumbo loudly. Noddy didn't dare to say anything more.

There wouldn't be much left of his little car if Jumbo began to bounce up and down in it. He hoped he would pay him for the broken eggs, but he didn't.

For two days after that Noddy didn't go to the ice-cream shop, and Mr Jumbo had to walk to the station. It did him good because he was much too fat.

But the third day Noddy went to the ice-cream shop again. He simply *loved* ice-creams! He had just been to the toyshop and had bought three balloons, one for Big-Ears, one for Mrs Tubby, and one for himself. He had left them on the seat of his car, as usual.

Mr Jumbo rushed out of his front door. Aha! Now he could ride to the station again. He didn't look on the seat, of course. He just sat himself very heavily down on those balloons.

BANG! POP! BANG!

All the balloons burst under him with a tremendous bang.
Mr Jumbo had a terrible shock. He tried his hardest to get out of the
car, but he was stuck fast.

"Help! HELP, I say! Noddy! Your car is blowing up! It's exploding!
It went BANG, POP, BANG! I shall be blown up too. Help, help!"

Noddy had heard the bangs and the yells. At first he was scared -
then he guessed what had happened, and he grinned all over his little
wooden face. Aha! Old Jumbo had sat on his balloons, had he!

He ran out. "Help me out, help me out!" begged Jumbo. "Your car's
going to explode. It's gone BANG, POP, BANG already."

"You're stuck," said Noddy. "I told you not to get in any more.
I think I'll leave you there. If the car is going to explode it will serve
you right to be in it!"

"I'll pay you anything you like
if only you will help me out!" said Jumbo,
doing a little bounce.

"All right. Pay me a shilling for my
butter, and a shilling for the eggs
you sat on," said Noddy. "Quick -
before another BANG-POP comes!"

So Mr Jumbo paid up with a groan,
and then Noddy tugged and pulled,
and at last Mr Jumbo got out.

"Is my tail still on?" he asked
anxiously. Noddy looked.

"Yes. It hasn't been blown off.
But don't you get into my car
again, Mr Jumbo. It doesn't
like you!"

And off went Noddy to buy himself
some more balloons. Dear me, you
should have heard him laugh!

THE END